Charles E. Martin

ISLAND RESCUE

GREENWILLOW BOOKS ▓▓ NEW YORK

Library of Congress Cataloging in Publication Data

Martin, Charles E., (date)
    Island rescue.

Summary: When Mae breaks her leg she is taken by boat
off the island where she lives to the mainland hospital.
1. Children's stories, American.
[1. Islands—Fiction. 2. Hospitals—Fiction.
3. Medical care—Fiction] I. Title.
PZ7.M356777Iq 1985   [E]   84-13672
ISBN 0-688-04257-0
ISBN 0-688-04258-9 (lib. bdg.)

TO MY SON JARED

It was just before spring vacation. Mrs. Gray was reading to the class from a book of poems. They loved it. She closed the book and said, "Now let's talk. We've said goodbye to winter. Now we say hello to spring. Heather, what are your thoughts about spring?"

Heather was surprised. She waited a moment and said, "Well, I feel warmer and happier."

"Thank you, Heather," Mrs. Gray said. She pointed to Hamilton, whose hand was up.

"I think about baseball starting this week," he said. Everybody laughed.

Mae said, "Flowers. I think about flowers, and lots of people and picnics."

They talked until school closed.

As they walked home, they talked about what to do the first day of vacation.
"Let's have a picnic," Mae said.
"A picnic just for us," Sam said. "That would be fun."
"Well, we'll need food," Hamilton said.
"We'll have to ask our parents," Rita added.
The parents all agreed, providing the picnic was in the woods and
not along the shore or on the cliffs. The food was to be a surprise.

The next morning everyone met at the library and started up the road.

"I hope they made baloney sandwiches," Hamilton said.

"Oh no," Lulu said. "Baloney is not good enough for a picnic. I'll bet they made toasted cheese."

"Ha, ha," Sam said. "It'll be cold toasted cheese. Yuck!"

A short walk took them to a clearing in the woods. It was a perfect spot and a perfect day for a picnic.

They had peanut butter and jelly sandwiches. Bacon and tomato. Cream cheese with walnuts and cream cheese with olives. Apples, pears, ginger cookies, chocolate cake, and carrot sticks. They were full.

After a while Mae went off to look at some flowers at the edge of the clearing. She took her wildflower guidebook with her. The others decided to play ball.

"It would be better with even sides," Sam said. "Where's Mae?"

"She's hiding. Let's go find her," said Hamilton.

"Ready or not, we're coming," they shouted.

But there was no answer.

"Maybe she went home," Lulu said.

They began tossing the ball around, but Jonathan kept on looking for Mae.

Mae had been looking at a clump of violets when she saw a baby deer. It bounded away along an old deer track and she rushed after it. But she missed a turn in the track and fell down some rocks onto a stone ledge. She couldn't get up. She cried, but no one heard her.

When Jonathan saw Mae's book at the edge of the trail, he followed the deer track. Branches got in his way and he pushed them aside. He was standing on the edge of a small cliff. Down below he saw Mae. He could see that she was really hurt. He ran back to the others, shouting for help.

Quickly, Jonathan explained what had happened. Sam said, "I'll get help. The Payntons. They have a phone."

"I'll come, too," Rita said.

"Call her mother," Kate shouted, as Jonathan led the way back to Mae. They comforted Mae as best they could. At last they heard the sound of a truck, and soon Harry and Sherm arrived. Sally Paynton had alerted the Coast Guard and Mae's mother.

"Broken leg, I think," Sherm said.

"Uh, huh," Harry said. "It is."

With a soft branch and some napkins he made a splint.

They carried Mae to the truck on a stretcher. Slowly and with great care, the truck moved over the bumpy dirt road. Jonathan and Lulu kept the stretcher from moving around. The others ran along behind the truck. At the dock a Coast Guard boat with a running motor waited for them. Mae's parents were already on the boat.

Quickly, the Coast Guard boat left for the hospital. The sea was smooth. The children waved goodbye. It was a quiet walk home.

Heather's mother said, "Don't worry. She'll be all right now."

When the boat docked at the mainland, an ambulance was waiting for Mae. In a few minutes they were at the hospital. Mae was wheeled into the X ray room.

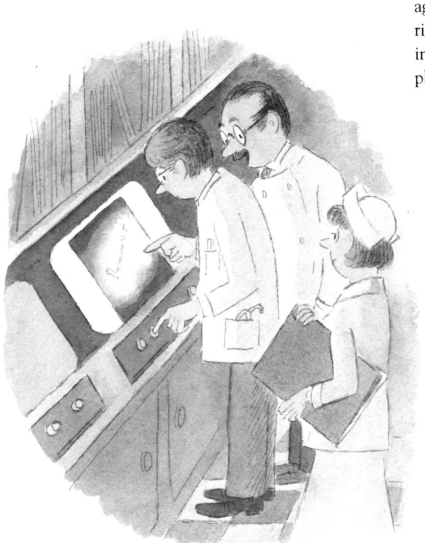

After looking at the X rays, the doctor agreed that Harry and Sherm had been right. Mae's leg was broken. In the operating room he gently set the bone back in place. The doctor put Mae's leg in a cast.

On the island, Mae's friends missed her. They sent her cards, but what they really wanted was to see her. Doctor Crane said they could all visit Mae for a short time, late on Sunday morning.

They brought gifts. They autographed her cast. They sang, "Get Well Fast," a song that Mrs. Gray taught them on the way over. They asked a million questions. They met the nurses and the doctors. Then it was time to go back.

PENN HARBOR HOSPITAL

Monday was the last day of vacation. There was a baseball game on Lighthouse Hill. Four of the older boys had joined in. There were quite a few Islanders cheering from the grandstand. The store truck came up the hill, and Sally and Mary supplied everyone with hot dogs and soda. During the sixth inning, Alfred Burton came up the hill and said that Mae would be on the one o'clock boat. The game was forgotten.

At one o'clock, everyone was at the dock. The sea was calm. The boat was on time. Mae was helped onto the steep gangplank. She hobbled up to the landing. Everybody cheered. Mae was home.